ISBN: 1494430533

ISBN-13: 9781494430535

D0113345

To my beloved kids

DEAR READERS,

Thank you for purchasing *Terry Treetop and the lost egg*

I really enjoyed writing about this little boy and his encounters with animals, and I've already had some great feedback from kids and parents who enjoyed the story and illustrations. I hope you too enjoyed it.

I appreciate that you chose to buy and read my book over some of the others out there. Thank you for putting your confidence in me to help educate and entertain your kids.

If you and your children enjoyed *Terry Treetop and the lost egg* and you have a couple minutes to now, it would really help me out if you would like to leave me a review (even if it's short) on Amazon. All these reviews really help me spread the word about my books and encourage me to write more and add more to the series!

Sincerely yours,
Tali Carmi

For one little boy, this summer was
going to be really exciting!
He and his whole family
were going out to do some camping!

This little boy is five years old,
and big trees he loved to climb!
His special name is Terry Treetop since
it is his favorite pastime!
Terry is very cute and chubby.
He has freckles and on his clothes
with patches over rips and tears
because always up the tree he goes!

When they arrived at the camp site,
Terry Treetop looked around
at the blue sea and the tall trees
and the green grass on the ground!

Terry immediately unpacked his bag
and got his binoculars out.
He spied something lying on the grass
and then he gave a shout!

"What is that little, white, round thing
lying under the tree?"
Then, he cried, "It is an egg!
Who owns this thing I see?"

"Who does this egg belong to?"
Terry curiously asked aloud.
"I promise to take you back home!"
to the egg, he vowed.

Terry got a small basket that
he padded with leaves to make a bed.
He gently placed the egg inside
and thought of a plan in his head.

He walked slowly to the rocky shore
until he came to the sea.
He saw a big sea turtle and
he asked very politely:

"Excuse me, ma'am? Is this your egg?
I found it on the ground."
The turtle had a big shell on its back.
It was green and brown.

"Oh, no!" the turtle then replied.
"That egg does not belong to me.
I have not lost one single egg,"
said the turtle named Sandy.

She told him, "All my eggs are here.
They hatch inside a little hole I dug.
Then they run to the water, though right now,
they are still in there, quite snug!"

Terry nodded his head sadly
and quickly said goodbye.
"I promised to bring this egg back home.
I promised I would try!"

So Terry kept on walking
towards a spring of sweet water
until he saw something long and brown.
It was an alligator!

"Excuse me, please," He softy said.
"Does this egg belong to you?"
The alligator looked at him and replied,
"I am Ally! How do you do?"

Ally was friendly, and she said,
"Let me look at it, just in case.
I'm sorry, boy, that is not my egg
because I hide them in a secret place!"

When my little gators hatch,"
Ally said while shaking her snout,
"I bring them to the water in my mouth.
That's how I carry them out.

When my babies are afraid,
into my mouth they run!
I protect them from bad weather,
strong rains and too much sun!"

Very sadly, Terry gave his thanks
and walked to sit on a brown log.
There was a pond beside it
where he met Fergi the frog.

"Hello, my name is Terry Treetop.
Could you help me out?"
He carefully showed her the egg,
but the frog said with a pout:

"I lay a chain of many eggs.
The one in your hand is not my own.
In the pond, my baby tadpoles stay
with me until they're grown."

From tadpoles, they grown up to be
a green frog just like me!
Look in the water. There they are!
They are lovely to see!"

Terry frowned and deeply sighed
as he went to search again
He walked back to the meadow
until he found Betty the hen.

"Hello there! May I ask a question?"
Then, Terry explained his task.
"I found an egg lying on the grass.
Is it yours?" He politely asked.

"I sit on my eggs to keep them warm,"
Mother Betty replied.
"When they hatch, they become chicks.
They follow when I go outside!"

They are cuddly and so cute.
My chicks are small, fluffy and yellow!
I'm sorry that I can't help you, Terry.
You look like a real good fellow!"

Sadly, Terry looked at the egg.
It looked so lost, so small and round.
"Who do you belong to, little one?"
But the egg didn't make a sound.

"We'll keep on looking, little egg!
Your mother must be full of worry!
I promised to get you back home,
so we had better hurry!"

Terry suddenly thought of something else.
"Was there something I didn't see?"
He used his binoculars again
to look back at the tree!

He saw a hole in the tree trunk.
Then, he made an amazing guess.
"The egg came from the tree up high.
It fell from a nest!"

Terry ran back to the tree,
and in the hole he saw
a nest made of twigs and branches,
some leaves and bits of straw!

Carefully, he placed the egg inside
then waited for its mother to return.
"I will stay here till she comes back,"
Terry said with so much concern.

So Terry patiently waited
and did not leave the egg alone.
"Don't worry. I'm here beside you.
I'll stay till your mother comes home!"

He waited for a long time.
He almost fell asleep.
Then, from the egg, he heard a sound,
so Terry made a little peep.

The little egg was hatching!
Then, Terry heard a tweet.
A little baby chick came out
looking so cute and sweet!

"Are you my mother?" It asked softly
with an adorable little coo.
Terry shook his head no and said,
"I am just looking after you!"

Make that little sound again!"
Terry told the little bird,
"So your mother can hear you
saying your first words!"

The little bird made another noise
and stepped out from the shell with a crack.
It looked to the sky. It chirped happily.
It saw its mother flying back!

Suddenly, Terry heard a flutter
of wings above his head.
Pipi the parrot landed in the nest,
and she happily said:

"My baby egg was lost, but now
I see he has been found!
I was so afraid that it was lost
when it fell on the ground!"

"Who helped my egg to get back home?
Who shall I give my gratitude?
Whoever helped us out today
must be so brave and good!"

Terry cleared his throat and said
with a big and friendly grin,
"I helped the egg to get back home.
What an adventure it has been!"

Mother Parrot was very happy,
and Terry felt just the same!
"I will always be here to help you!
Terry Treetop is my name!"

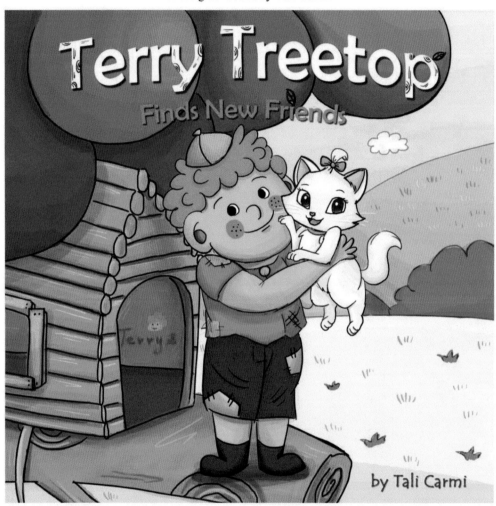

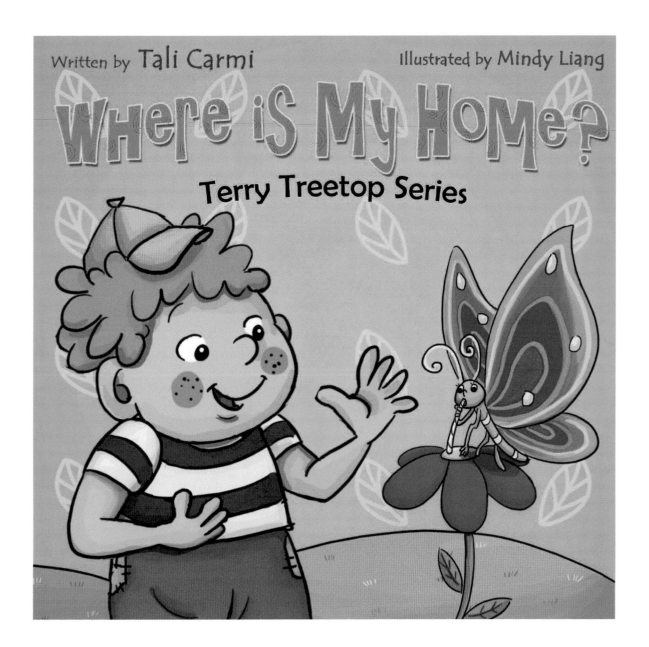